STAR WARS®
EPISODE I

Watch Out, Jar Jar!

by
Kerry Milliron

illustrated by
Bob Eggleton

A Random House Star Wars® Storybook

Random House  **New York**

© 1999 Lucasfilm Ltd. & TM. All rights reserved under International and Pan-American Copyright Conventions.
Published in the United States by Random House, Inc., New York, and simultaneously in Canada by Random House of Canada Limited, Toronto.
Used under authorization. First Random House printing, 1999.

www.starwars.com
www.randomhouse.com/kids

Library of Congress Catalog Card Number: 98-83057
ISBN: 0-375-80028-X
Printed in the United States of America   10 9 8 7 6 5 4 3 2 1

Jar Jar Binks has a way of getting into trouble . . .

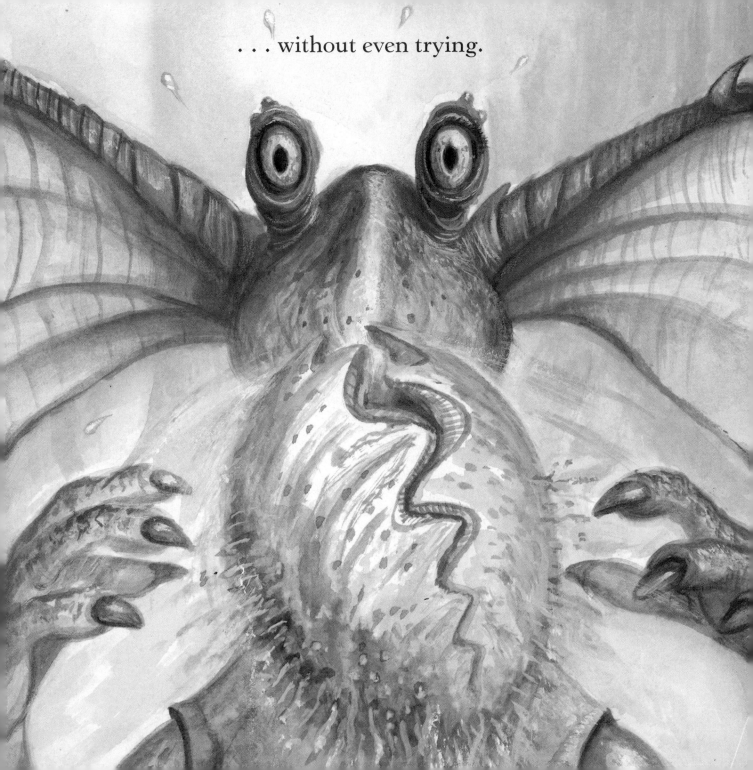

. . . without even trying.

When frightened swamp creatures stampede, Jar Jar's tasty breakfast is rudely interrupted. WATCH OUT, Jar Jar!

Jar Jar wonders why all the animals are fleeing. Then he sees the huge Trade Federation transport speeding toward him. "Oh, noooo!" cries Jar Jar.

Jar Jar grabs hold of the first thing he sees. Luckily, the first thing he sees dives into the muddy swamp, taking Jar Jar along with him!

"Ooh, I luv yous," Jar Jar wails to the Jedi Master Qui-Gon Jinn. "Yousa savin' my life."

WATCH OUT, Jar Jar!
As a battle droid swoops down, Qui-Gon quickly draws his humming lightsaber. In a flash, he destroys the deadly droid. "Dis crazy!" Jar Jar cries. "Whas goin' on here?"

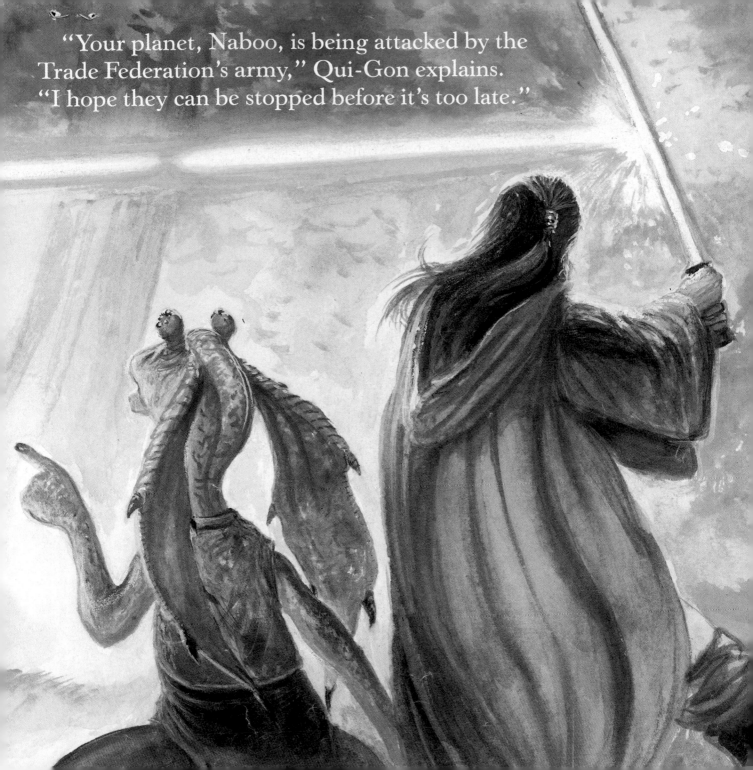

"Your planet, Naboo, is being attacked by the Trade Federation's army," Qui-Gon explains. "I hope they can be stopped before it's too late."

"Mesa stay with you," insists Jar Jar. "Now wesa friends for all days. Forever and forever!"

"What?" Qui-Gon asks in confusion.

"Because yousa savin' my life," Jar Jar tells Qui-Gon, "mesa owes you a life debt."

Qui-Gon agrees to let Jar Jar stay with him. But the Jedi Master cannot always keep Jar Jar out of trouble.

WATCH OUT
for the opee sea killer, Jar Jar!

WATCH OUT
for high waterfalls!

WATCH OUT, Jar Jar!
Never make a Dug angry.

And never, ever stick out your tongue near a Podracer!

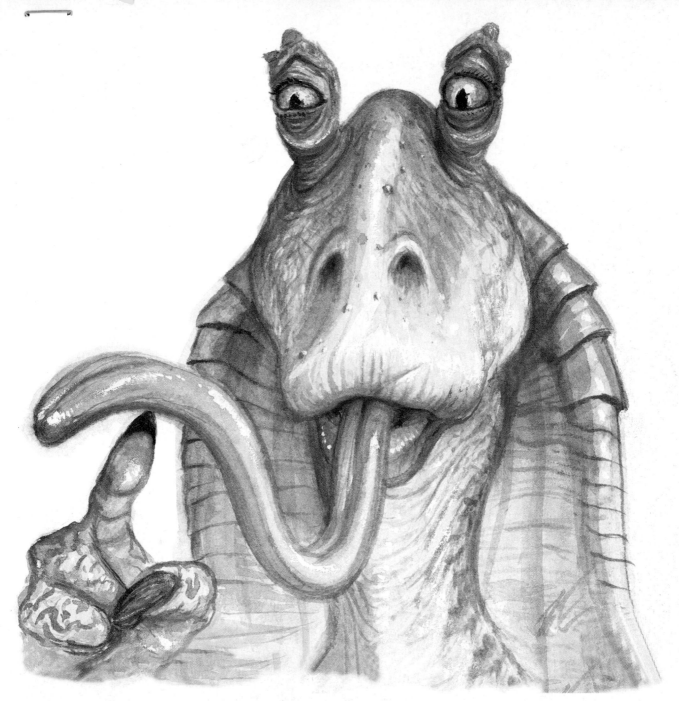

"Ouch time! Why mesa always da one?"

WATCH OUT!
Droids are very delicate.

Jar Jar knows he is clumsy, but he doesn't mean any harm.
He is always quick to help out when he can.

Jar Jar knows that if anyone needs help, it is the Queen of Naboo. She must stop the Trade Federation army of battle droids from hurting her people.

Jar Jar wants to help Queen Amidala. "Mesa Gungan tribe got a grand army," he tells her. "Wesa help da Naboo fight."

Jar Jar takes his friends to the Gungans' secret hiding place. Boss Nass is the Gungan leader. He listens carefully to the Queen and agrees to help her fight the Trade Federation army.

Jar Jar is pleased. But it's a big surprise when Boss Nass turns to him and says, "Mesa has grandest good job for you, Jar Jar."

Jar Jar is made a Bombad General to help lead the battle!

WATCH OUT, Trade Federation!
Battle droids are no match for Jar Jar!

WATCH OUT, destroyer droids!
Jar Jar can wipe out a whole platoon with his Gungan energy balls.

When the battle is over, Jar Jar is a hero.
"Yousa grand warrior!" declares Boss Nass.
"Tis nutten," mumbles Jar Jar. "Tis nutten at all."